YUCK!

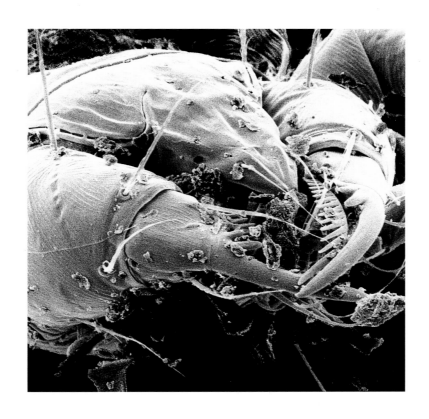

...hi mom, I'm home

written by robert snedden

For Alice: my very own micromarvel

Simon & Schuster Books for Young Readers
An imprint of Simon & Schuster Children's Publishing Division
1230 Avenue of the Americas, New York, New York 10020

front cover: David Scharf/Science Photo Library; back cover, left: Manfred Kage/SPL, center: Dr. Jeremy
Burgess/SPL, right: Andrew Syred/SPL; page 3: Dr. Jeremy Burgess/SPL; pages 4-5: SPL; pages 6-7: Dr. Tony Brain
and David Parker/SPL; page 8: David Scharf/SPL; page 9, top: M.I. Walker, others: David Scharf/SPL; page 10:
Andrew Syred/SPL; page 11, center top: SPL, center: SPL, bottom left: SPL, bottom right: Andrew Syred/SPL,
background: Manfred Kage/SPL; pages 12-13: M.I. Walker; page 14, left: CNRI/SPL, right: Biophoto
Associates/SPL; page 15, top and center: M.I. Walker, bottom: SPL; page 16: Dr Jeremy Burgess/SPL; page 17, left:
M.I. Walker, center left: Dr. Jeremy Burgess/SPL, center: Vaughan Fleming/SPL, right: Dr. Jeremy Burgess/SPL; page
18: Manfred Kage/SPL; page 19, left and center: David Scharf/SPL, right: Dr. Tony Brain and David Parker/SPL;
page 20 Ralph Eagle/SPL; pages 20-21, bottom, page 21, left and right: Dr. Jeremy Burgess/SPL, center: David
Scharf/SPL; page 22: David Scharf/SPL; page 23, bottom left: Andrew Syred/SPL, others: Dr. Jeremy Burgess/SPL;
page 24: David Scharf/SPL; page 25, left: CNRI/SPL, top right, center right: David Scharf/SPL, bottom right: Dr.
Brad Amos/SPL; page 26: Andrew Syred/SPL; page 27, left: BSIP, VEM/SPL, center left (and top of flap): Andrew
Syred/SPL, center right and right: Manfred Kage/SPL; page 28: top, Professors P.M. Motta, K.R. Porter and P. M.
Andrews/SPL, bottom: Professor P. M. Motta/Dept of Anatomy/University 'La Sapienza', Rome/SPL;
pages 28-29: Richard Wehr/Custom Medical Stock Photo/SPL; page 29, bottom left: CNRI/SPL, right Hans
Jesse/Robert Harding Picture Library; page 30, top left and right: Dr. Jeremy Burgess/SPL, bottom left: SPL, bottom
right: David Scharf/SPL: page 31, top left: David Scharf/SPL, bottom left: SPL

Designed by Mike Jolley

Printed in Hong Kong

First Edition
10 9 8 7 6 5 4 3 2 1

ISBN 0-689-80676-0
CIP data for this book is available from the Library of Congress

YUCK!

A big book of little horrors

. . . how close can you

The microscope is a powerful tool. It can reveal unexpected things about the most commonplace objects. If you could look really closely at something ordinary, like a pin, what would you see?

The first of our pictures shows the point of a pin around 10 times its normal size. It still looks like a pin, doesn't it? Let's get a little closer.

The second picture is about 100 times normal size. We can see now that the tip of the pin isn't a sharp point and the surface isn't as smooth as we might expect. And what are those yellow splotches?

In the third picture the pin is magnified over 800 times. Would you ever have guessed that this was a pin at all? We can see clearly now that the yellow splotches are made up of many tiny individual specks.

The fourth picture, around 6000 times life-size, reveals a thriving colony of rod-shaped bacteria living happily on the point of the pin. Colonies of bacteria such as this are everywhere, even in the cleanest homes. The final picture is more than 35,000 times normal size!

The pages that follow hold even more yucky surprises in store. If you really want to know what's in your home, turn the page…

If you dare!

1

2

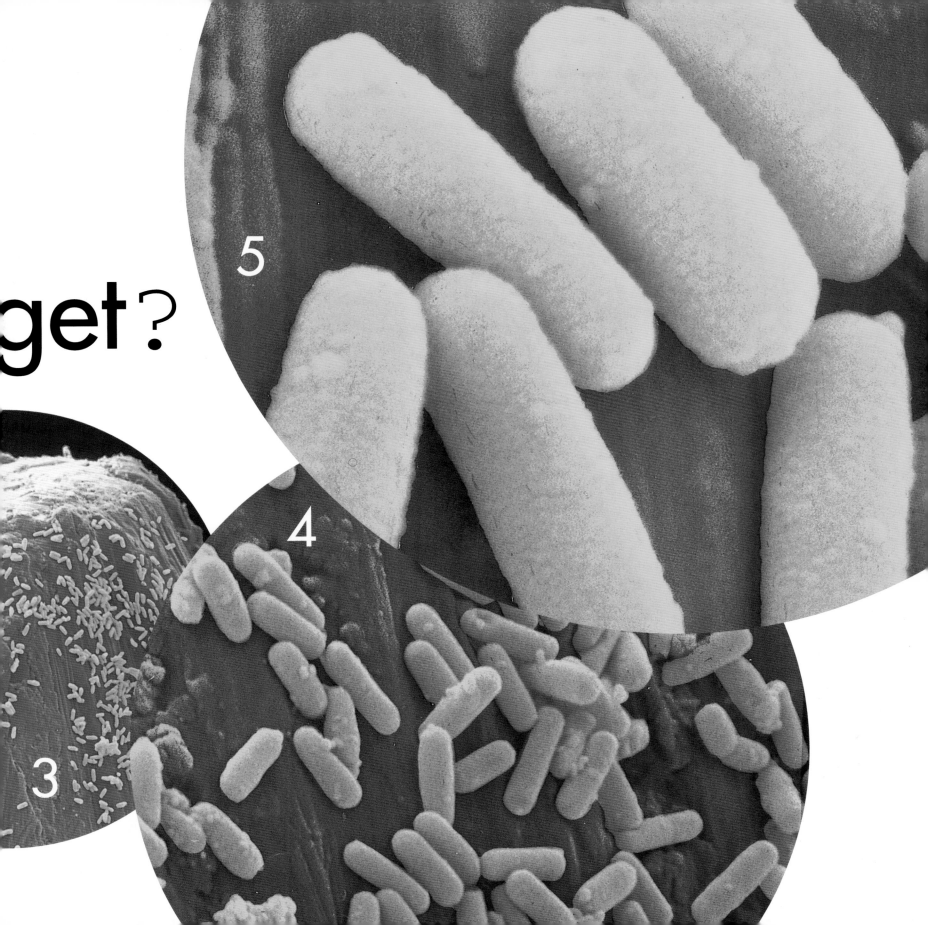

get?

5

4

3

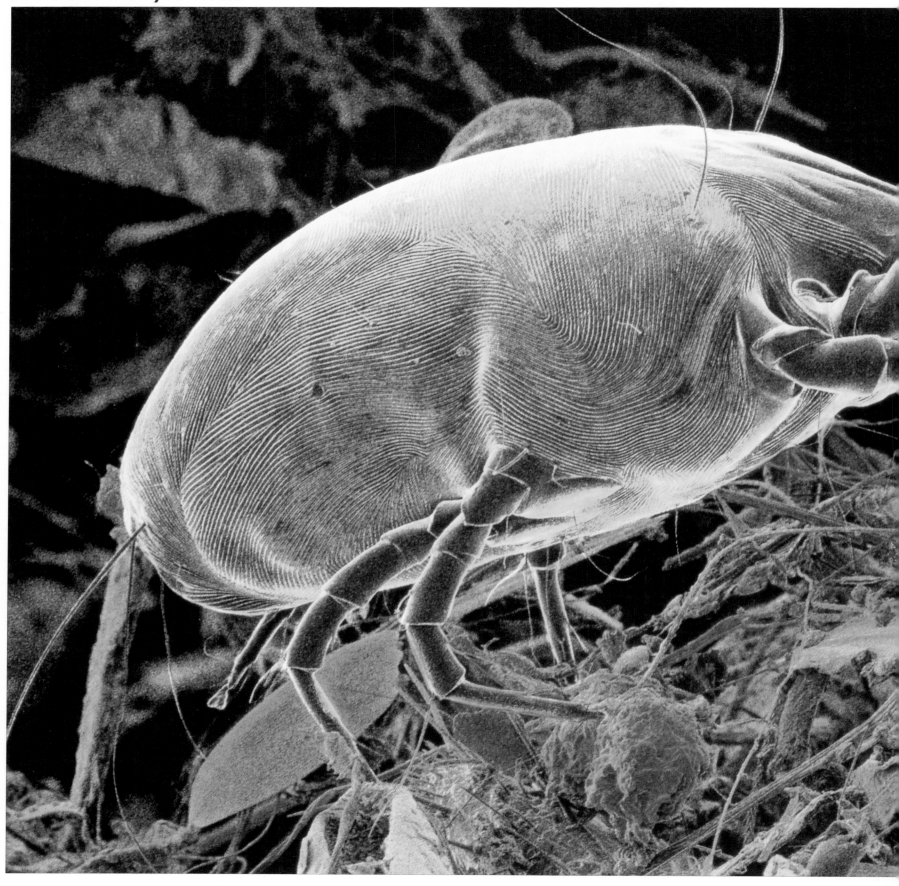

feeling clean?

It's good to feel clean isn't it? There are all sorts of things you can use to clean up the house, your clothes, and yourself. And you would never think of using anything dirty to clean up with, would you? For instance, how would you feel about sticking these giant, grungy fenceposts in your mouth? Probably not very happy. But you may be surprised, because...

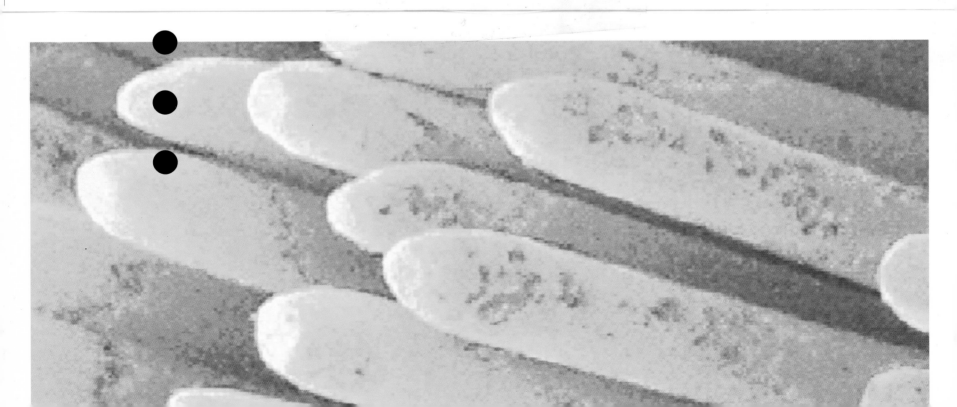

could you eat...

What in the world could this be? Is it a photograph of a bizarre extraterrestrial landscape sent back by some far-ranging space-probe? Could that be a mighty glacier moving in from the right? And what lurks at the bottom of the mysterious caves in the surface of this alien world? Can you guess what its secrets might be?

are you hungry?...

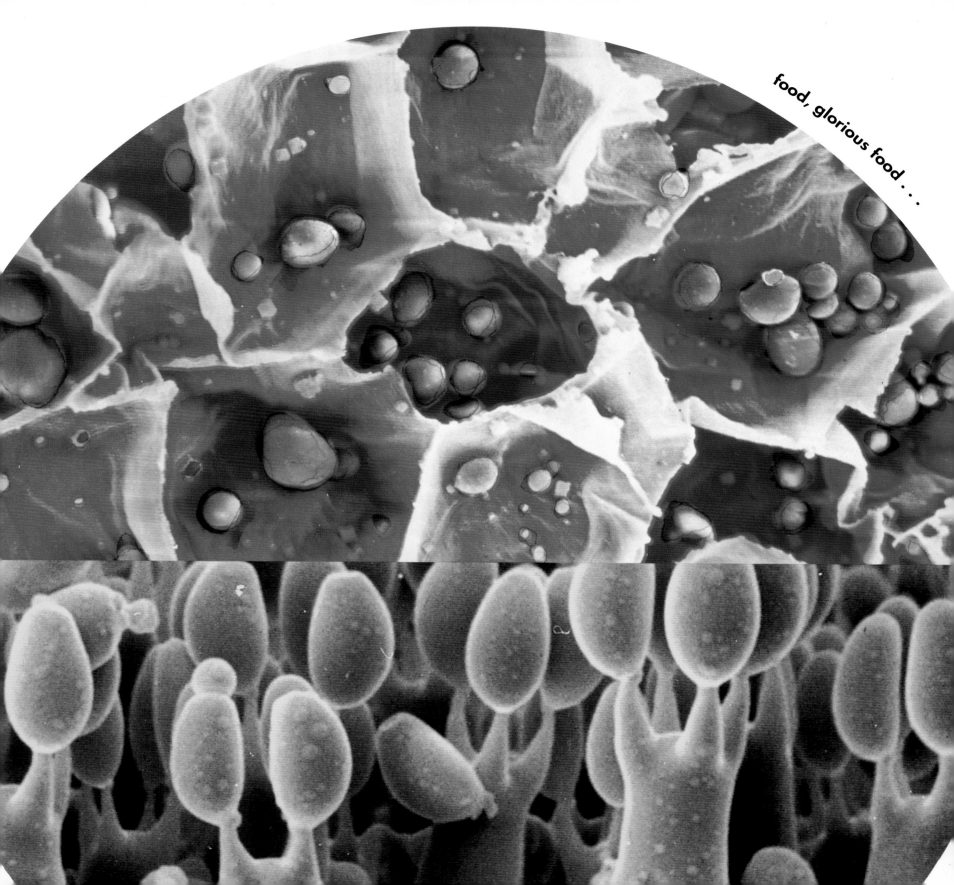

food, glorious food . . .

fresh from
the ground • • •

Just imagine. It's been a long time since you had your yucky breakfast and you're hungry

again. "That's alright," says a helpful person. "I'll dig something up for you."

Then he gives you a plate of stuff that looks like a horrible collection of

assorted insect eggs! Are you going to eat it?

Or are you just going to say **YUCK!**

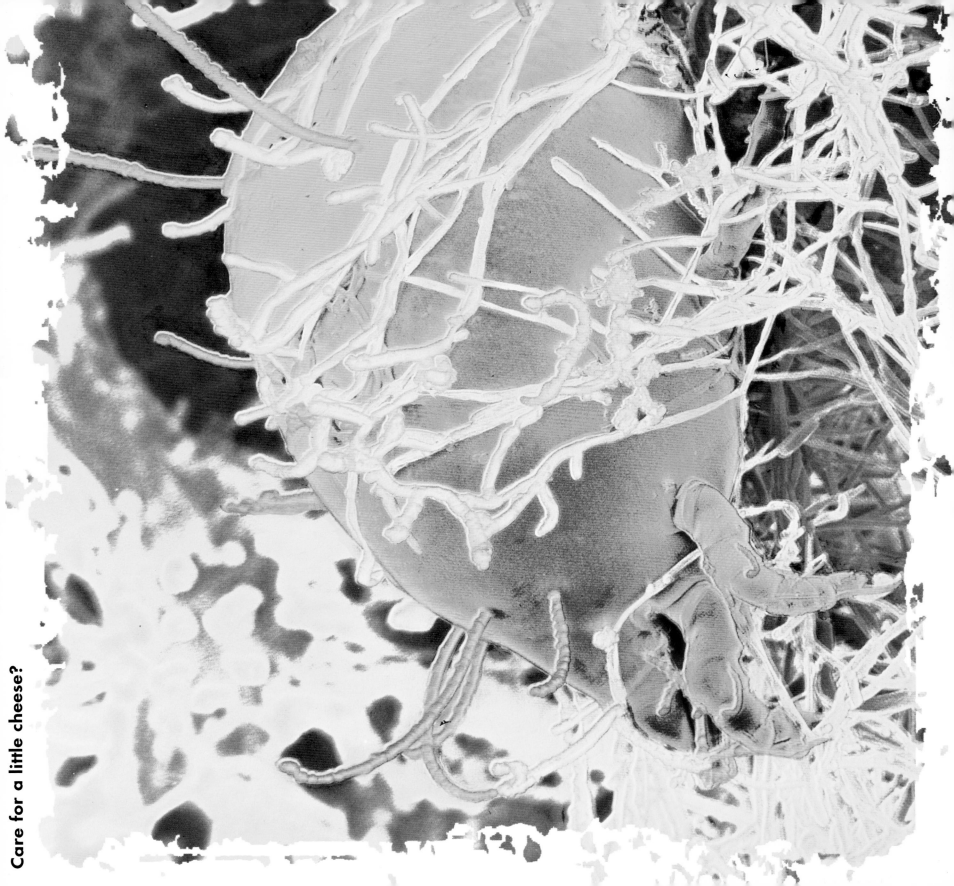

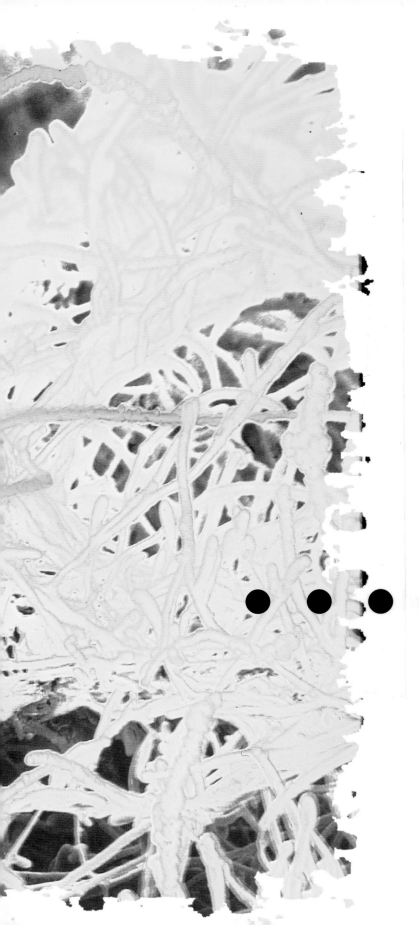

The handsome orange fellow in the middle of the picture is a mite, like the dust mite we met a few pages back. There might very possibly be a few like him in your kitchen. Mites like this like to roam around looking for suitable bits of your food to eat. In particular they head for things that might be a little past their best. Like the moldy cheese this mite is feasting his way through. It's not just mites that will get to your old food. The clue is in what got to the cheese before the mite…

. . . . . these things could grow on you!

Are you looking at me? . .

. . . . . . with the darkness comes

In the dark places of your home there is always something lurking. Scurrying here and there, they feel their way with long antennae that twitch constantly. They like the kitchen best because there are many dim, damp corners to hide in and there is plenty to eat. If you go into the kitchen tonight and turn the light on quickly you might just catch a few of your uninvited guests. If you're brave enough, that is, to come face to face with…

animal, vegetable or mineral . . . ?

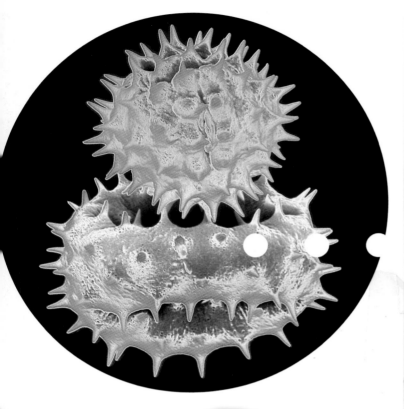

• frankly fantastic!

The wonderful thing about the microscope is that it can show you aspects of the world you probaby never dreamed of. It's difficult to know just what it is we are looking at here, yet what you can see are different parts of very special living things. They are commonly found in every garden and many people bring them into their homes because they appreciate their beauty. Can you guess where these science-fiction creations have come from?

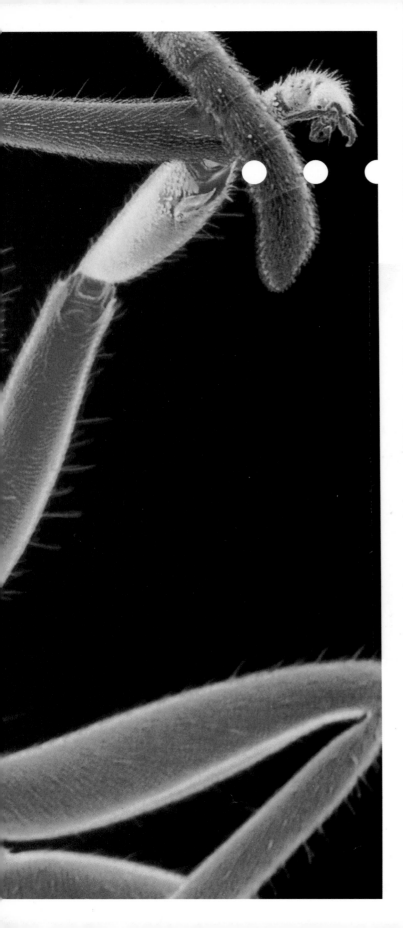

the aliens are here!

Like a monster from a science fiction movie, a strange creature rears up as you approach. Its antennae twitch restlessly as it searches for the telltale chemical signals that mean food. The fearsome mandibles around its mouth open and close menacingly. This alien is only one among many, an entire alien nation is here right now and they are...

care for a

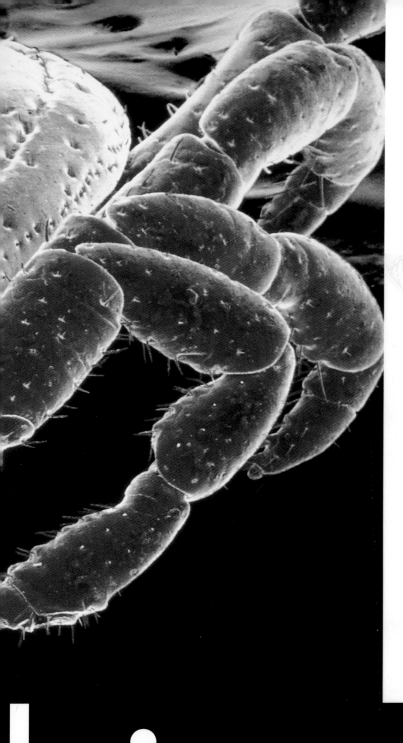

It is a law of nature that, unless you are a plant and can make your own food, you have to eat. Some animals eat plants, some animals eat other animals, and some animals just eat parts of other animals. This charming creature is after blood. He'll bore right in and stick there until he's had his fill. Make no mistake, he'll be hard to get rid of once he gets attached to you. He won't kill you, but he and others like him could make life rather unpleasant for you and your pets…

bite ?....

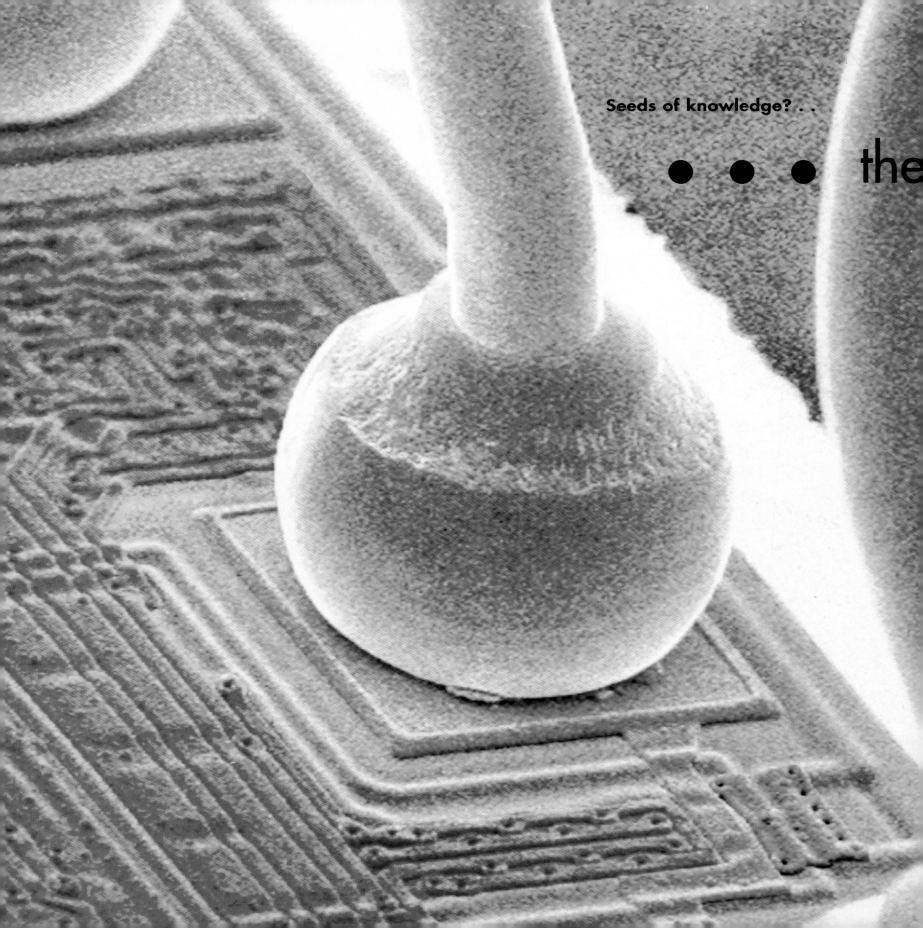

Seeds of knowledge?..

● ● ● the

world of the living . . . .

When we step into the microscopic world we are
entering unknown territory. You may
see things you've never seen
before, or see things you
thought you knew
well become
strange and
baffling. What
do these
pictures show?
Is that a strange
sprouting seed?
What are those
colorful party balloons
beside a meaningless
collection of blue blobs?

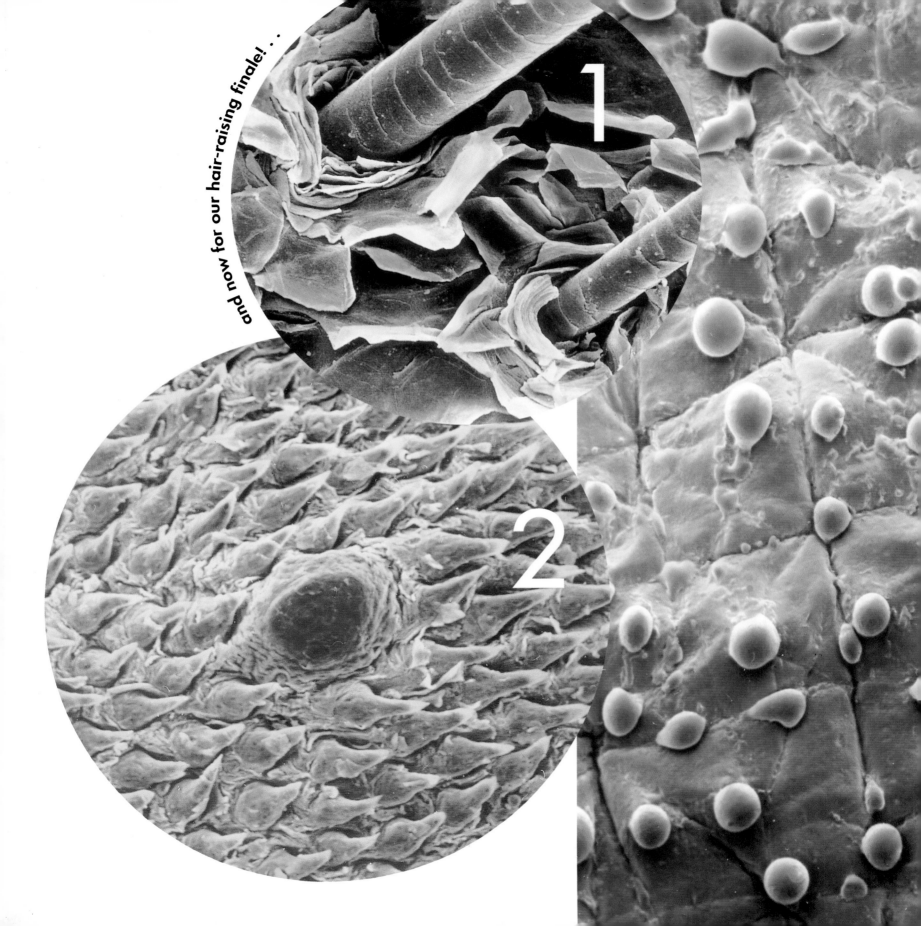

and now for our hair-raising finale! . .

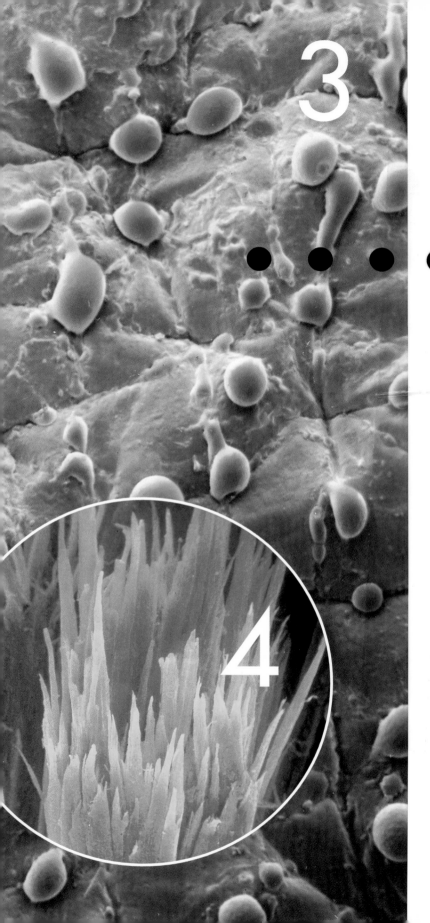

....what is the yuckiest thing of all?

These colorfully yucky scenes have something in common. They're not aerial photographs of deserts, seashores, and other habitats, or parts of a flower. They're not silicon chips, optical fibers, or other bits of electronic wizardry. Here is a clue. They are all found on something that's warm, sensitive, active, hairy, busy, and noisy. It's...

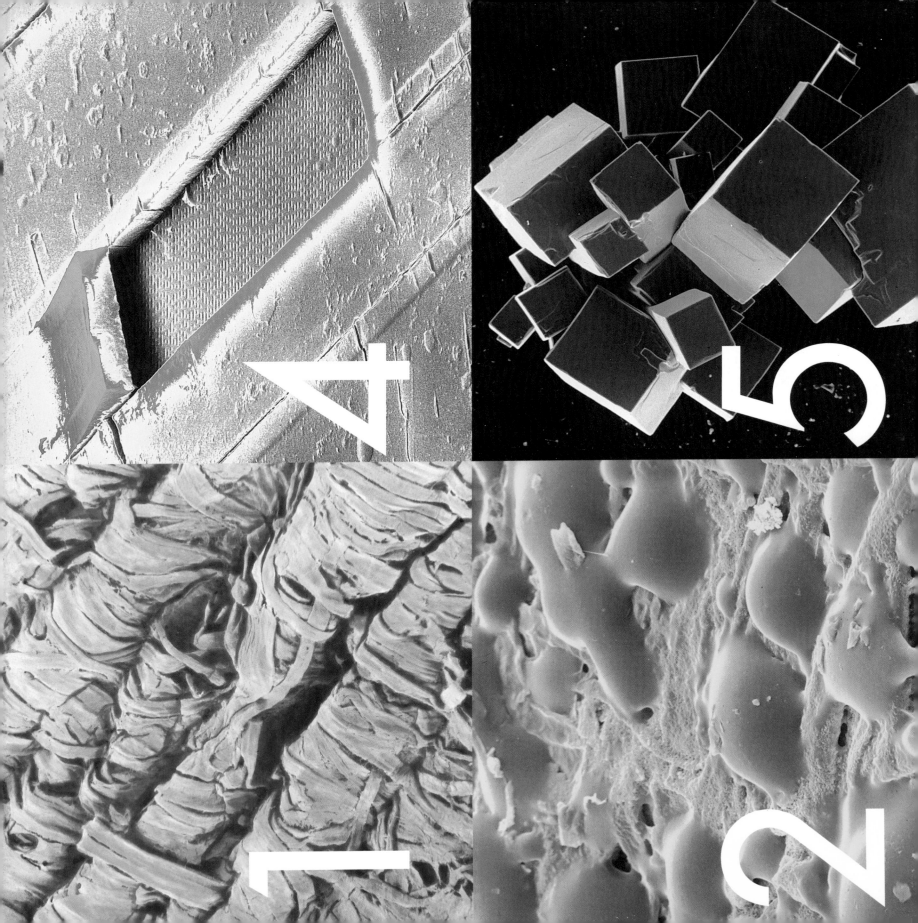

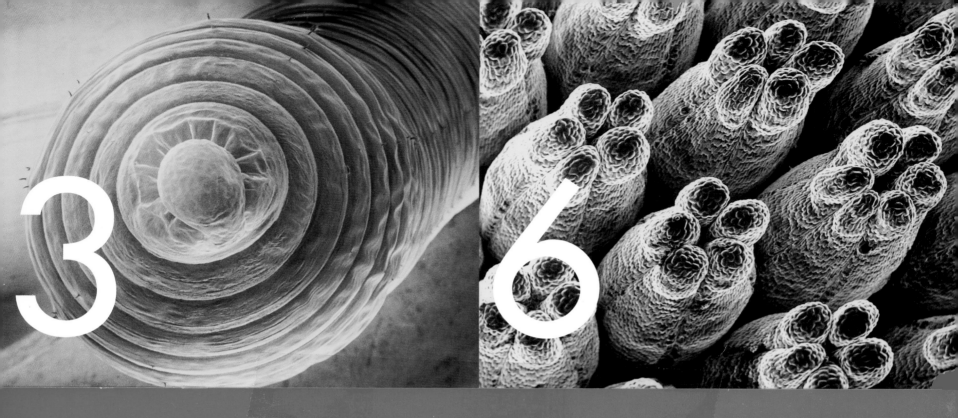

3

6

what is it?

It's quiz time! Here are six picture puzzles to test you. How good are you at solving microscopic mysteries? Here are a few small clues. You've seen one of these things before in a different view and two are from the living world!

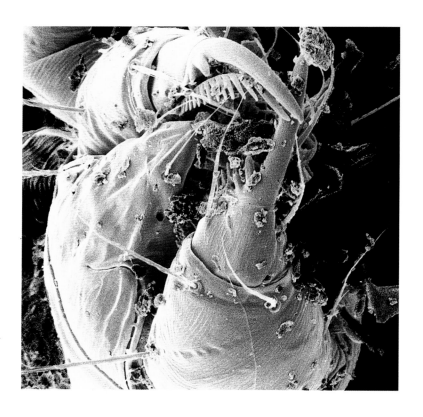

...I'll be back!

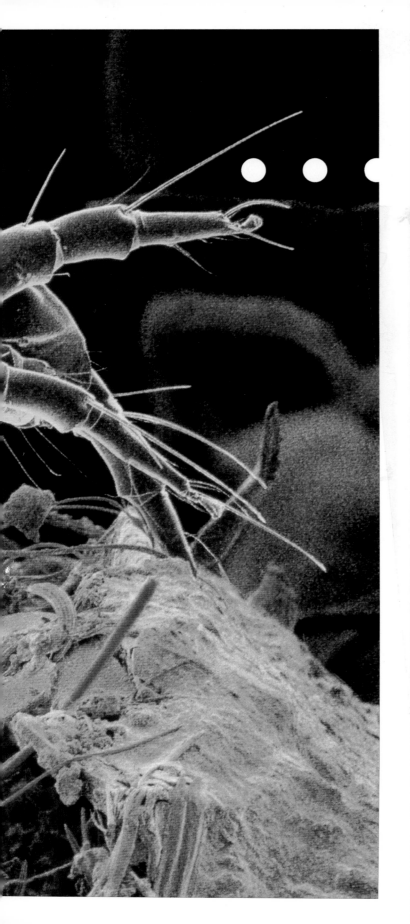

. dust-up in a dust ball

If you spot some dust around your house you probably think, Time for a clean up! But wait a second, is it just dust that you're getting rid of? Would you believe that you're disturbing this fellow here and maybe a few thousand more like him? Now this doesn't look like something you would want to upset, does it? Except that there's more here than meets the ordinary eye. We're going down the microscope into a dusty world...

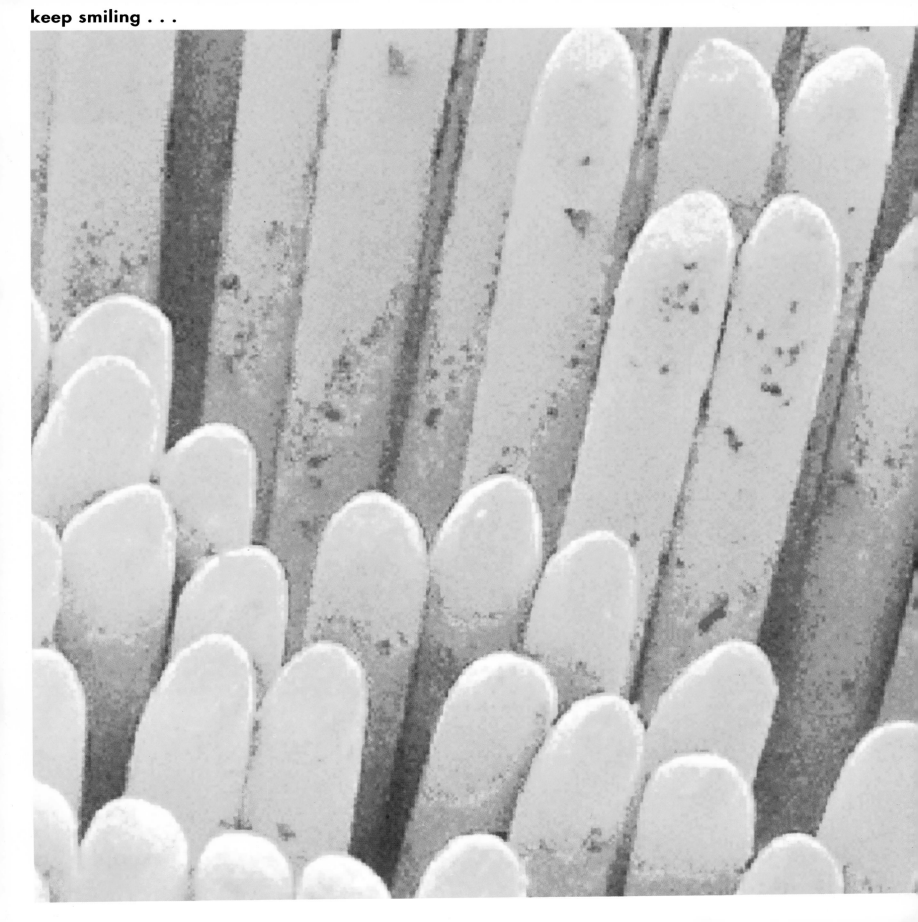